# EMILY BROWN
and
# FATHER CHRISTMAS

To TUESDAY, WITH LOVE from HER GODMOTHER, C.C.

FOR BETSY, ERICA, SADIE and FIZZY, N.L.

HODDER CHILDREN'S BOOKS

First published in Great Britain in 2018
by Hodder and Stoughton
This paperback edition published in 2019

1 3 5 7 9 10 8 6 4 2

Text copyright © Cressida Cowell, 2018
Illustrations copyright © Neal Layton, 2018

The moral rights of the author and
illustrator have been asserted.
All rights reserved.

A CIP catalogue record for this book
is available from the British Library.

ISBN 978 1 444 94200 2

Printed and bound in China

Hodder Children's Books
An imprint of
Hachette Children's Group
Part of Hodder and Stoughton
Carmelite House
50 Victoria Embankment
London, EC4Y 0DZ

An Hachette UK Company
www.hachette.co.uk

www.hachettechildrens.co.uk

# EMILY BROWN and FATHER CHRISTMAS

written by
## CRESSIDA COWELL
illustrated by
## NEAL LAYTON

Hodder
Children's
Books

# Once upon a time,

there was a little girl called Emily Brown
and an old grey rabbit called Stanley.

One Christmas Eve, Emily Brown and Stanley had hung up
their stockings and were reading each other a story, when there was
a "HO-HO-*HELP*!" coming from outside the window.

HO-HO-
HELP!

It was Father Christmas, hanging by a rope from the roof.

"Oh Emily Brown, Emily Brown!" cried Father Christmas.
"Could you possibly call the fire brigade?"

"I can do better than that," said Emily Brown, getting out her Emergency-Rescue Machine. Stanley pushed the button to **ON**, and together they **SU-U-U-CKED** Father Christmas in through the window.

"Why thank you, Emily Brown!" said Father Christmas.
"I don't understand how that could have happened!
I'm using the very latest climbing equipment …"

"Dropping down the chimney magically might be better," said Emily Brown.
"Sometimes the old ways are the best ways."

A little while later, after Emily Brown and Stanley had politely pretended to be asleep while Father Christmas filled their stockings, there was another "HO-HO-*HELP!* HO-HO-*HELP!*"

This time it was coming from the roof.

"Oh Emily Brown, *Emily Brown*!" cried Father Christmas.
"I don't understand it, but my sleigh has broken down ... It's the
most up-to-date sleigh you can get. It has turbo-whatsits and
jet-thingummys and I turned that switch there but it went

# BANG!

And now it won't move."

PHUT
PHUT PHUT
PHUT PHUT
PHUT

JOYS

"Flying reindeer might be better," said Emily Brown.
"*They* never break down."

"Yes, but they're not very modern," said Father Christmas.

"Sometimes the old ways are the best ways," said Emily Brown.
"Luckily, Stanley keeps a few flying reindeer in the wild bit at
the bottom of the garden just for Christmas emergencies."

Emily Brown and Stanley put on their winter warmers and went down to the wild bit at the bottom of the garden to find some flying reindeer for Father Christmas's sleigh.

"Thank you, Emily Brown," said Father Christmas. "I really am most terribly grateful."

"It's no problem," said Emily Brown and Stanley, waving him goodbye. "Being kind and helpful to others is what Christmas is all about."

Quite a long time later Emily Brown and Stanley were fast asleep, when they were woken by a "**HO-HO-*HELP*! HO-HO-*HELP*!**"

Emily Brown and Stanley were so very, very tired …

… but they opened their weary eyes and they staggered onto their sleepy feet and they put on their winter warmers and they struggled out into the snow.

It was Father Christmas again! And he was in quite a tizzy.

"Oh Emily Brown, Emily Brown!" said Father Christmas.
"I have iPhones and why-phones and flashing screens
with buttons, but I find them all terribly confusing,
and so far I've only got to the end of the street!
And I've got to deliver all these presents to every child
in the whole entire world before tomorrow morning …
What am I to do?????"

Emily Brown looked at Stanley
and Stanley looked at Emily Brown.

A Christmas day with **NO STOCKINGS**! There were going
to be some VE-RY disappointed children out there …

It was time for some firm words.

"Father Christmas," said Emily Brown, very sternly.
"There is only one way to do this, and that is by **MAGIC**."

"Magic isn't very modern!" wept Father Christmas. "I don't want to be out-of-date and out-of-touch … But some children have written asking for 'peace to the world' and 'sweet dreams forever' … and I can't find **THOSE** in any of these catalogues … and … and …

# A-A-ATISHYYOOOOOOO!"

Father Christmas was getting very upset.

"Leave this to Stanley and me, Father Christmas," said Emily Brown. "All this trying-to-be-modern has tired you out and I think you're coming down with a nasty winter cold."

So Emily Brown and Stanley tucked Father Christmas up with a cup of hot chocolate and some warm slippers in the chair in front of the fire.

"Stanley and I don't think you need to be up-to-date, Father Christmas," said Emily Brown. "We love you just the way you are."

"Oh, that's so very kind of you," sneezed Father Christmas, gently falling asleep.

"Okay, Stanley," said Emily Brown.

"This year the children of the world are depending on US."

Emily Brown and Stanley took out their dream catchers and they looked at their star maps, and off they flew in Father Christmas's sleigh to deliver presents to every single child in the entire whole world, even though it was way past their bedtime.

And they did it by MAGIC because it
may be old-fashioned but it's a *lot quicker*.

SANTA
STOP
HERE

When they got back
Father Christmas
was fast asleep.

So Emily Brown and Stanley very, very quietly put a few little presents in Father Christmas's stockings, which were hanging on the edge of the chair, without waking him up.

And then Emily Brown and Stanley went to bed.

And a lovely old-fashioned star hung over Emily Brown's house that night.

Because being kind and helpful to others is what Christmas is ALL about.